3 Watersoaked Murders
Alicia
Zenia
Maria

Alicia = a woman is found drowned. It is learned that she was working against an international group trying to gain power by manipulating banking

Zenia = A woman, a popular local entertainer, is recruited to help fight the international banking group

Maria = a murder on the comarca. About gold? How stupid!

Contents

About the author

CD Moulton has traveled extensively over much of the world both in the music business, where he was a rock guitarist, songwriter and arranger and in an import/export business. He has been everything from a bar owner to auto salvage (junkyard) manager, longshoreman to high steel worker, orchid grower to landscaper, tropical fish farmer to commercial fisherman. He started writing books in 1983 and has published more than 350 books as of January 1, 2023. His most popular books to date are about research with orchids, though much of his science fiction and fantasy work has proven popular. He wrote the CD Grimes, PI series, and the Det. Nick Storie series, Clint Faraday series, and many other works.

He now resides in Gualaca, Chiriqui, Panamá, where he writes books, plays music with friends, does research with orchids and medicinal plants. He has lately become involved in fighting for the rights of the indigenous people, who are among his closest friends, and in fighting the extreme corruption in the courts and police in Panamá.

He offers the free e-book, *Fading Paradise*, that explains what he has been through because of the corruption.

CD is the discoverer of the Chadam Protocol for curing cancer.

Facebook page Ambrosia peruviana for cancer.

<u>One</u>
Alicia

<u>*Introducing Tony Vega*</u>

Antonio (Tony) Vega M. (for Martinez) sighed and maneuvered the boat to the dock, where he would have to wait at least half an hour before he could get fuel.

Oh, well. He was used to it. He could spend the time finding out what the locals were up to. He liked to keep up to date on some things. He had been a cop here in Panama for 18 years. From walking a beat to a bicycle, to a motorcycle, to a car – when he was promoted to Specialist Detective in Homicide and Violent Crimes.

He was actually pretty good, but retired when he had the opportunity. Crime was getting out of hand, and the corruption in the police and courts was just too much to fight. Too many mobsters, local as well as Colombian and Mexican. He couldn't live with what he had to submit to, in a moral sense, if he continued.

He had done the regular tours of duty all over the country. He liked Bocas del Toro, the archipelago, very much. He liked the island life (except Isla Colon, which was just another Caribbean tourist trap) more than the interior, though he loved the mountains and, unlike most cops here, loved the Indios. He had taken the time and effort to learn about their culture, and saw how misunderstood they were.

Silvio Smith (A lot of the Indios had names from the tourists who were their Grandfather or such), said that the drowning of that English woman just didn't seem ... right. It couldn't have happened the way they said. Not there.

Tony understood how the Indios thought. They had, at times, uncanny ability to find an oddity in what seemed a natural occurrence.

It seemed a part-time resident in Punta Robalo had been swimming, the way she did almost every day, and had some kind of cramp or stroke or something and had drowned. There were several other people close, but no one noticed anything out of the ordinary. A young boy had felt her body with his foot and looked down in the crystal clear water to see the body. They had dragged the body out onto the beach and called the police, who said it seemed like a cramp or stroke or something.

"Stroke?" Tony asked. "How old was she?"

"Oh, maybe thirty five or forty. Not many have strokes until they are seventy or eighty."

"No marks of violence?"

Silvio shrugged. "How would I know? I wasn't there."

"Then why do you say it didn't seem right?"

"Other people. If she had a cramp, she would yell or something, and they were there. She was too young to have a stroke. She swam every day, so she knew how.

"It just isn't ... right."

Tony thought, then nodded. "I see what you mean. I'll look into it."

Tony talked with several other people. Two of them

knew about the drowning, but said it happened.

He got the fuel, then headed around toward Isla Colon. The fueling station was in Almirante, on the coast.

He thought a little more. He didn't have much to do, and this one might be interesting – and it would be handled through Chiriqui Grande, not Isla Colon. He headed that way.

"Her name was Alicia Gayle Morton," Sergio Valdez, Chief of Police in Chiriqui Grande, said. "She had a house just out of Punta Robalo, and a finca on the carretera. Never heard much about her, except when she reported a burglary at her house a couple of months ago. People liked her a little, or were neutral, or thought she was a little too judgmental of the Indios.

"I noted that it was a bit odd, but she always swam away from the others there, and was not very, what you would call, gregarious. Sort of a loner.

"We do not have any reason to be suspicious."

"Probably okay, but I'll do some checking. Can I get into her house, or is it cleaned out and inherited or whatever?"

"Just nine days. It will not be touched until heirs take over, I suppose. The court instructions said not to do anything more than watch to see no one tries to steal anything."

Tony nodded. "I can get access?"

Sergio thought. "Not really, the way it was worded. If you ... if you were told something was seen that was supposed to be in that house? Perhaps a piece of jewelry you were suspicious about, so came to me?"

"Serg, we're old friends, and you know I'm retired police, but there was a rumor that a Rolex watch that belonged to a, what was the name? Alice Morris? The woman just out from Punta Robalo. Gringa or Ingles or something. A hood in Changuinola was trying to sell it. I would like to ask her if she was missing it?"

"You amaze me with the information you can get! I have to inform you that the woman suffered a fatal accident, but considering that such an item may be missing would suggest there has been an illegal entry to the place. That cannot be permitted.

"I feel there is a suspicious circumstance. I cannot allow you to enter the property ... alone. Perhaps I can accompany you to the place and we can make an official report, if that is suitable?"

"Certainly!"

They went to the police cruiser and headed for Punta Robalo.

"Sounded official enough for you?" Sergio asked, when they got into the cruiser. "You saw me turn on the recorder. You know how that works. Our asses are covered."

Tony grinned and nodded.

The house was a neat, small cabina-type structure. a pale blue color with windows and doors framed in natural wood. It was attractive and clean. The yard was well-kept.

Sergio turned on the body cam and opened the front door. "Nothing in the first room seems disturbed, and the door showed no signed of having been forcefully opened.

Nothing seems amiss here."

They went into the hallway. "The doors to the rooms on either side are open. The room on the left is a bedroom. Everything seems in good order. The closet is closed. Upon opening, I noticed that here seems to be the first place anything is not completely in order, though it could be natural, in the way we often leave things that are out of sight in less careful order. Several items of clothes are on the floor, and ... Tony Vega, who is accompanying me here, is searching the hat shelf, where there is some disorder.

"Tony?"

"Things were moved here. There are four hat boxes that are opened. They contain, three of them, rather odd types of hats. I see the one is from Jamaica, and one from Mexico, and one from Guatemala.

"I guess she kept hats as souvenirs when she visited other places.

"The box from Brasil contains papers. This one is a receipt for office supplies from Office Center, in David. This is a receipt for computer repairs, also David. This is for a copier from El Poderoso, in David.

"She seems to have done a lot of shopping in David.

"Here are several receipts for various items held together with a paper clip. All from Panama City.

"Here are several, also held with a paper clip, from Puerto Armuelles.

"Here are three from Bugaba.

"Serg, all these were held with paper clips. Where is the clip for the David receipts? It's not in the box.

"All these are for office things or computer ... Four eight gig memory sticks?

"Serg, I think we need to find her computer. I think someone thinks she had something, found these papers, and went for the computer."

Sergio pointed to his watch. Tony continued: "We came because of a Rolex watch. I think we've found something a lot more important than an expensive piece of jewelry!"

"We have?"

"Thirty two gigs on memory sticks? A likely search for papers? That translates to memory in today's world. I want to know a lot more about this Alice woman! I want that computer and those sticks!"

"Her name was Alicia. I, too, wish to know much more about her and what she was doing, I think.

"Shall we find that computer?"

Tony nodded. They went to the room on the other side of the hall. It was a guest bedroom. Totally normal.

The end of the hall was in the kitchen. There was a bathroom just before. It had been searched.

The kitchen had also been searched. It was mostly a very professional job ... with certain exceptions.

"Serg, two people have searched this house. One was professionally complete, the other not so professional and incomplete.

"Let's find that computer. The door to the left is to the laundry room, so the one to the right should be ... ah! Her study and computer room! Whatever they were searching for was here. It's a mess!"

They went into the room and spent more than half an

hour looking for anything that could tell them, or even hint at, what was the object of the searches. Sergio took fingerprints, after saying he knew no one would leave prints in this kind of situation. Everything was wiped.

"Tony, we haven't found one single memory stick. I think, perhaps, we are a day late and a balboa short!"

Tony was at the computer. He found the hard drive was erased.

"I have one very small hope. It's based on the fact she had those receipts hidden in a hat box in a closet in another room.

"Maybe the fact there were two searchers is something in our favor."

"You do? It was?"

"Yeah. What we're looking for will be hidden in something common in another room."

"What are we looking for?"

"A memory stick."

Sergio looked thoughtful, then grinned a dry grin, and nodded.

Tony turned on the printer.

"There won't be anything there," Sergio suggested. "The computer's erased." He turned off the body cam recorder with a sharp look to Tony, who nodded and punched the "tools" button. There was no legend on the computer screen, of course.

"I'm going to guess. If it's like mine, it will be the third one down." He punched the down arrow two times, then hit enter. The printer activated and printed a few paragraphs.

"There are a number of lines still in the cache from the last thing printed. Let's see what we've got."

He turned off the printer and the computer, then took the paper to read:

... when the shipment didn't arrive. We knew that they were onto us. We need instructions. We are hiding at the Castillo place, but they will know where you are.

The project can't collapse now! We are so close! You have to get Samuels to move on the political end! He will not take instructions from anyone but you! He can use the corruption we are fighting to expose some of them. It is better than nothing. We can stop some of it and build publicity and a base to attack the rest.

Can you have Samuel get in contact with us with your instructions?

Fast, Alicia! It has to be fast! They have forced us to defend, and that is not a good position!

Can you make your contact sign an affidavit? If they learn who he is, they are not beyond killing him, as we all know only too well. All we know about him is that he is a fat moreno, so we cannot expose him, which is good.

Fast, Alicia! It must happen fast!

"What in the hell have we stumbled into here?!" Sergio demanded.

"We have a hint. I think, just maybe, that we're going against corruption in very high places. As this says, they'll kill you without thought if they think you're a danger!

"Be damned careful, Serg. Don't let anyone even guess you might be involved!"

"Let's see if the little lady left us a memory stick. I think it would have been found, but I retain a little positive hope!"

They went into the kitchen to look through all the hiding places they could think of, then into the laundry room.

"It will have occurred to the professional searcher to look here," Sergio said. "We can but hope that the lady was more clever than the searcher."

They found nothing.

They went back to the sala, where Tony carefully scanned the room, then went to a little end table to pick up a cigarette lighter in a topaz base.

"She didn't smoke, and there's no ash tray. Why would she have a lighter? It's not the type for the stove, and that would be in the kitchen."

He studied the lighter, then pulled it out of the base. There was a tiny memory chip – two of them – under the lighter.

Sergio grinned. "That's our Tony Vega, master detective!"

Let the Chips Fall

"It would seem that our search of the premises of Alicia Gayle Morton found some evidence that a search was made by an unknown person or persons. Certain items, computer memory sticks, were missing, and the computer was erased. There were no usable fingerprints and no samples that would be useful in DNA charting. We have a cryptic few lines from the printer. Investigation will continue when and if other evidence can be located." Sergio said, and turned off the recorder to raise an eyebrow at Tony.

"We can't let on that we found anything," Tony warned. "I think that, just maybe, we can add a murder charge to them – if we can find them."

Sergio pointed to the door. they went out to stand in front of the station.

"What do we have, really?" Tony asked.

"Hopefully, these chips will give us enough information," Sergio replied. "We can tie it into a conspiracy charge if we can garner enough information from them. I hope it is information that can be used."

"If it wasn't, she'd still be alive."

Sergio nodded. "We cannot read these on the computers here. That would be ultimately stupid."

"I have my laptop on the boat. Shall we go fishing?"

"Yes. I'm off direct duty for a few hours. I think I would

like to, as you say, go fishing."

"Yeah. Rigged for sharks and bottom feeders."

They went to the dock and onto Tony's boat, then headed out Eastward toward Cusapin. Tony pointed his lips at a boat that left the docks just after they did. "Your office bugged?"

"It would appear. That is why I did not want to discuss anything inside.

"What do we do to make them think we have nothing"

"We fish for awhile. It will confuse them."

They rigged and started a slow troll. Tony took the camera from the console safe box and adjusted the zoom, then turned enough that it would look like he was photographing Sergio with the follower in the background, too far away to identify. He watched the zoom to see that the boat was *The Angelena*, and that the two in it were not locals. One was watching them with binoculars. After a few seconds he showed Sergio the pictures.

"The light one is from Venezuela. I know nothing about the other one.

"Tony, I have been thinking about the paper in the copy machine. I have a pale idea about something.

"There was mention of a moreno gordo. I have a suspicion that it is about Gordo Serano. He is a shady character in Changuinola, known to associate with known criminals, who never trust him because he uses cocaine and talks too much. There is also a suggestion he uses blackmail."

"So. He collects information and proof for the blackmail, so could supply Alicia with information?

"We'll have to have a chat with him!"

"No. I thought of that. It is why I think he was murdered three days ago."

"Shit!"

"That would cover it."

Sergio got a strike. Tony maneuvered until they had the sixty pound yellowfin tuna aboard.

Sergio pointed to the followers, who were heading back toward Chiriqui Grande. "They figured we actually were just fishing ... well, we were. Too."

Tony laughed. He set the automatics to continue on a trolling pattern and speed and took the laptop from the safe box. Sergio gave him the chips. He put one into the adapter and brought it to screen.

The first clip, *GV*, was at a birthday party for a little girl, about 5 years old. It showed the various guests, which meant nothing to Tony, but Serg said it was most interesting. The heavier man was Javier Guerra, a top judge in the circuit court. He had seen the man he was talking to somewhere.

Tony paused the scene and brought up a series of pictures on split screen. Number seventeen was the man.

"He's Paulo Vasquez, suspected land fraud, has wife and two daughters. Lives near Boquete. Prosecuted four times, but ruled insufficient evidence every time."

"So. Continue."

Vasquez reached inside his shirt and handed Guerra a package that was wrapped like a present.

"I'd say about eighty thousand, if it's in hundreds," Tony suggested.

"It would appear odd that the father of the person the party is for would give a gift to a guest, would you say?"

Tony grinned and gave him the finger.

The next clip, *HA*, was in a restaurant. Tony and Sergio both said, "Donaldo Herrera!" at the same time. A woman walked past the table, and there was suddenly a small package on the table.

"Sylvia Arrends," Sergio said. "Secretary to Jorge Ramos, suspected of fraud and manipulation of accounts involved in money laundering. We could never get enough evidence to prosecute."

"So! Chief Investigator Herrera has a small box surreptitiously deposited on his table by the secretary of another suspected crook. Interesting."

"Is it not! Do you know who that man at the table behind Herrera is?"

"Of course. He was recently a police officer for the fraud division in Tole. He was removed when he shook down an Indio who was selling yuca. The vendor stall man photographed the whole thing, as he didn't like Herrera, because he tried to shake him down. Carlos Camacho."

"I'd bet there was a lot more than one doing the blackmail bit. He dead yet?"

"No. He would know better."

Tony nodded, and brought up clip *GL*.

On a bench in a park of some sort. Javier Guerra was sitting, reading a newspaper. A man came to sit beside him. He said "Buenos," and ignored him, otherwise. The man got up, talking on a cell phone, after about a minute and a half. There was a thick envelop laying on the bench, which Guerra slipped into his briefcase. He got up and walked away.

"Who is he?" Tony asked.

"I don't know, but will soon. I will know where to look."

The next clip was *SL*. It was at a crowded disco. It showed a black man with dredlocks dancing with a pretty morena. They danced into another couple, and moved away. Sergio shrugged, then said to back up.

The woman they ran into had a purse on her shoulder, which was unusual. The black slipped something into it, as shown in slow forward plays.

"I don't know who she is, but he is a Jamaican man suspected of being in the drug trade. Jerome Silah. I can possibly learn who she is. I know her name starts with an S."

There was an extension on that one. It showed the woman going into the courthouse.

"I'd say to find which judge or cop she works for," Tony said. "That's the pattern here." Sergio nodded.

There were six more clips, much the same. They featured police captains and judges, mostly, but one, Z, seemed to be something else. It was just a man walking around the streets in Isla Colon, Changuinola and Chiriqui Grande. He was one of the men on the follower boat. The Venezuelan.

"I wonder!" Sergio exclaimed. "I wonder greatly!"

"Uh-huh. Did she have a clip featuring her killer?"

They put the other chip in the reader. It was mostly accounts about the people investigating. It did have a couple of lists – one of which was names and locations and dates of the clips on the other chip. Z was Arnaldo

Zamorra.

"Perhaps our investigation of these chips has proven fruitful!" Sergio cried. "It has, at the smallest part, given us a few things to investigate further!"

"Can't argue with that!"

They spent some time going through everything, then Tony put the chips in a small evidence bag, thought, made copies of the chips, then replaced them in the bag. He slipped his copies into a small compart-ment hidden behind the safe box – after adding the shots from his camera to the one with video clips.

They headed back to Chiriqui Grande, where Tony gave the tuna to some friends at the dock, with the guarantee he and Sergio would have a good meal as part of the deal.

That went without saying!

Back at the station, Sergio found the Venezuelan's records. Arnaldo Zamorra Mendez. It seemed he was there as a refugee, though he had been to Panama several times in the past.

"How did he get refugee status?" Sergio asked. "He was under suspicion for three years. Suspicion of laundering money for the Cali Cartel – the idiot cop asked as he investigated corrupt Panamanian officials."

Tony laughed. "Ain't it the truth!"

"Hmm. His records from Caracas suggest he was suspected of being an enforcer for a Peruvian group of less than honest businessmen. So this idiot policeman would ask how he ever got the original travel passport, and certainly how he got authorization to come to Panama. There are ten reasons a visa would be refused in these superficial notes.

"Tony, we are up against something that is dangerous beyond what we may suppose. I will understand if you, a retired policeman, would decide to not, as you say, 'Sink the boat.

"We say 'Rock the boat' – but you may be more accurate. Let's go for it."

They shook hands.

"Tonio, I want to look at some reports ... here in the files ... about the investigation at the scene where she died. Routine things. I think I saw something ... here it is!"

He read a few pages, then handed one to Tony.

... a large dark man with a lot of gold chains and some fancy rings and one of those phony Rolex watches. He drank a Malta, I think. He tried to get me to talk to him, but he looked like a thug, even a scar on his cheek, and I'm not about to get involved with that kind of cholu ... then there was a girl, Lena, who...

"I want to know a lot more about Zamora. That's a description that fits like a video record!" Sergio said sourly.

<u>Going for It</u>

Tony looked at the three attractive women who came to his house to "Discuss certain matters." They were dressed as Jehova's Witnesses, and were carrying Bibles.

"Sr. Vegas? We are not what we look like. We are known as the three G's. I am Gina Castro, this is Gilda Sanchez, and this is Gloria Quintera.

"We were working with a woman who was murdered. Alicia Gayle.

"May we speak with you, in a very secure private place?"

"I'm not interested in your silly babble, but you can come in and try to convince me of something or other," Tony replied. He pointed his thumb at the newel on the stair rail, and did the silent thing with his finger across his mouth and stood aside for them to come inside. When they were inside and the door shut, he said, "It can't pick up what you said with your back to it. I'm supposed to be such a stupid detective that I didn't find it ten minutes after it was put there, more than a year ago. I've sent a lot of whoever they are on some strange wild goose chases.

"I do want to know a lot about Alicia and what you're doing."

"Alicia was the fourth of our little religious nut quartet," Gina replied. "We called ourselves GAGG. We are investigating corruption in the justice system of Panama – as a superficial search will show. We have even been successful in two cases. We got two beat cops convicted of shaking down tourists!

"Of course, we don't know what to do with these hundreds of videos of most of the rest of them doing worse. We're just some nutcase cult members, out to save the world from itself.

"Believe it or not, we couldn't care less about crooked beat cops or the crooked courts – except in a very limited number of cases, where they have connections with others. From Venezuela and Colombia and Argentina."

She seemed to have a rather superior attitude, and managed to sound condescending. Tony decided he didn't much like her.

"Why have you contacted me?"

"Because we were asked to coordinate a few things with you, as you're working with the police. Sergio is too honest for us to use him."

But you figure I'm not honest? Well! "Well, he was very good at finding who killed Alicia."

That shook her! "He *did*!?"

"Well, we found a thing on the printer that hadn't been erased from the cache. He said he had asked some questions, privately, about her killer – like how and why he was ever given a visa to enter Panama – so it was pretty obvious."

"But ... but ... *who*?"

"Zamora. Isn't that about as obvious as anything could be? A known hit man, illegally in this country, under investigation by her, and she's knocked over? He's in the area, and within a few hundred meters of her, minimum, when she died? I mean, surely you didn't miss *that*!?"

"But ... he was there?! You are sure?"

"He got a Malta at the refresqueria about half an hour before she was killed. Finding that was a matter of asking the girl at the refresqueria. He is rather ... distinctive."

She seemed very shaken. "I'm not ... are you sure? Could it have been someone else?"

"Only if he has an identical twin, complete to the scar on his right cheek."

"We'll have to ... I'm confused! He is working with us!"

"Gina! This is crazy! He's your boyfriend! What's ...?!" Gilda cried. "Alicia always said she didn't trust him as far as she could throw a two ton weight!"

"So. Has it seemed that they were always a step ahead of you in your investigations?" Tony asked.

Gina put her fingers across her lips, shook her head, and opened her purse to take out a small compact. She pointed at it and at her ear. Tony took it and opened it, lifted the powder puff, and use a fingernail to take a small battery out of the case.

"You three find some place he can't get to you! Fast!"

"He's right outside," Gina said. "I have a pistol. We all do. He's experienced in using one. We're not."

"I am," Tony said. "What's it really about?"

Gloria said, "South America. They're going to consolidate everyone there through the banks. They represent the actual owners of the banks, and can manipulate the economies of almost any country in the world.

"Well, not Venezuela, and that's why we trusted Zamora

, in the first place."

"They couldn't pull it off!" Tony cried. "That's fantasy land!"

"In five years, they think they can. We're fighting that. I'm from Brasil, Gilda's from Argentina," Gloria said. "It's why food and medicines are blockaded from going into Venezuela. The government will fail, and they will establish a central bank there. That will give them control of the entire continent. Thousands, if not millions, will die. It's an old story."

"But it's the USA that's blockading ... so. It's true."

"There was ever a doubt?" Gina asked. "I think we'll be among the first killed, at this point. They're professional. We won't be able to get word out, and we can't leave anything that would ever be found."

"They thought that about Alicia," Tony said, drily. "Come on. We'll leave them a puzzle, if only for a very short time." He went into a closet and opened up the wall in back. He pushed them through, and closed the panel from the back side. He sealed the panel carefully so it couldn't again be opened from the apartment. They were in another closet in the adjoining apartment, which was unoccupied at the time. They went out onto the balcony over the alley in back, where he dropped a rope ladder. They went down quickly, then he pulled a slip-knot and rolled the ladder up. He dropped the ladder into a garbage bin by a picnic table. They went into the forest and down to the ocean, where he took a cayuca with a small motor from the mangroves. They crossed to a little puebla on the peninsula, then hiked across to Tierra Oscura, about an hour and a half. Tony got the water taxi from there to Puerto Armuelles. Six hours later they were in a small café near Potter Town. The women said they knew a person who would get them to Ojos de Aguas, where no one would look for them. They had a way to escape from there.

Tony took the bus to Chiriqui Grande.

<u>Scary Position</u>

"Sergio, I have it all, right here." He handed the mini-cassette player to Sergio, who would make several copies of the tape. "Is Zamora where we can get to him?"

"Yes – unless he's as professional as he wants people to think."

"He is. A lot more."

Sergio got the walkie-talkie set from his desk and called Number four. "He's meeting with Guerra and Vasquez in Boquete. They seem to be waiting for someone."

"We have to be able to get several of them at once. We're in a scary position here. These are international hoods with financing from people who think nothing of dropping a billion here and there.."

That got him a very strange look. "No, I'm not drinking, and I'm not coked up. If my sources can be believed, this is a lot bigger than we're equipped to handle."

"Should I get in touch with the CIA?"

"They're the last ones you want to get involved – more than they already are."

"One of their fantasy land screw-ups?"

"No. They're being used, if they're involved at all."

"Tony ... what are you saying?"

"Listen to the tape."

Sergio shrugged and went into the office. Tony said not to listen to it in the station.

"I don't think the station can be bugged very effectively."

"When we *know* there are top officials in the policia in it?"

Sergio looked shocked, and nodded. They went to a little café the police spent a lot of time in. Sergio rolled his eyes, and they left. "This would be easier than the station. I think I don't want to use the cruiser, either."

"Shall we take a stroll toward the bay? We can check on what the aduana has coming through."

Sergio lifted an eyebrow. They turned at the corner toward the docks. "Serge, talk without moving your lips much. Act like we're just chatting. Use the earphones on the cassette."

The walked slowly toward the docks. Sergio mumbled noises quietly, and Tony replied the same. By the time they got to aduana, Sergio had heard the whole tape. Just before they went in the gate, Tony slipped the mini-tape from the cassette and replaced it with one that had a lot of jumbled noise, with an occasional sentence or two that could be heard. He put the real tape in a shielded box. He told Sergio he expected a try to get the tape, or to erase it.

"Erase it? How?"

"It's magnetically stored on a cassette. It's damned easy to erase it. The same way they erase the ID strips in the markets. With a strong magnet. A magneto you can carry in a little briefcase can erase anything within twenty feet or so."

They went into the offices and asked to see records of what was found the last two weeks on ships from Puerto Rico. That would completely confuse anyone who thought they would be looking for evidence from any other place. They puttered around for about half an hour, then went out. A drunk was by the door, and staggered against Tony. Tony grabbed his hand and twisted his arm behind his back. The cassette fell to the sidewalk.

"Hmm. Pickpocket. Attempted personal robbery. Good for ninety days. You're under arrest, Snookums."

"Man, I don't know what you're talking about! I just accidentally ran into the guy! You planted the tape ... whatever it was on me!"

"So drunk you staggered into me, then are cold sober thirty seconds later?" Tony said. "I think we need to interrogate this one. Is he local?"

"No. I saw him twice before. He was talking to that big Venezuelan."

"The one who killed that girl? Drowned her?"

"Uh-huh."

"Accessory to murder premeditated?"

"Uh-huh."

"Eep!" the "drunk" squeaked.

They took him to the station and booked him on the personal robbery charge, "With other charges to follow."

"You aren't going to question him?" Tony asked.

"Why? We know what he'll say." He pointed to the door. They went to stand just outside. "I want to see who makes his bail," Sergio said. Tony nodded. They went to Tony's office to wait. Fifteen minutes late a lawyer came to post bail. Tony told Sergio to have that lawyer followed by someone who would not be noted easily.

"Serge, the lawyer was being followed. Why?"

"I saw that. I have no idea, unless ... Tony! We have to follow him! He knows who sent him to bail Florentino out!"

There was a screeching of brake around the corner. They ran to see the lawyer laying under the wheels of a truck carrying vegetables to the market.

"My god! That guy was pushed right out in front of me! I swear, I couldn't stop! It was too close!" the truck driver cried.

"Did you see who pushed him?" Sergio asked.

"Some guy with a blue shirt! I didn't see who it was, just that he pushed him!"

Tony looked up to see the follower – in a green and yellow shirt. He smirked at him. The guy turned and walked away, looking back with a scared look on his face.

"Let him go. I think maybe we'll get a call from someone," Sergio suggested. Again, Tony nodded.

They waited until the ambulance and traffic cop came, talked for a few seconds with the cops, telling them the guy was pushed, and it was too close for the driver to stop. They were surveiling another person, and saw it. The person they were following used the confusion to get away. They could only give a very small description. The pusher was average, in a lot of ways, and his back was to them at the time, so they couldn't see his face.

They went back to the station. An old Chinese woman was waiting for them.

"Captain Valdez? It is imperative that I speak with you and Officer Vega." She pointed to the light fixture.

"About what?" Sergio asked, rather impatiently.

"I have three mini-supers, and someone is stealing things and breaking things."

"Where?"

"Just past Rambala. They told me you would have to handle it. They said you would know about the black flower they leave. That you had done a case with the voodoo phony stuff, so you would know who they were." She kept pointing her thumb at the door. "I have my car and driver. You won't have to use the police car, so they won't know I came here."

Sergio nodded very slightly, and they went out to the waiting car. Rather slowly. The woman used a cane, and seemed to have a problem with her right leg.

When they were in the car and driving away, she straightened up and seemed to lose fifteen or twenty years.

"I'm Mae Lum. I'm with the International Resistance Front. You have become involved with a very serious threat to stability of the Central and South American countries. I know who you are.

"It seems three of our minor operatives are in hiding, and one is dead. You found who committed the killing. Even we were greatly surprised to find that Zamora character was as big a shot as he is.

"They are planning to use Panama in some kind of international blackmail scheme. They have some very powerful people here in their pockets.

"You can see how big it is. China is involved in this way. The USA can't be trusted, as they've already corrupted many of the top politicians and judges.

"Your involvement is accidental, and you've got them

confused and more than a little afraid. If they are exposed now, they may fail.

"They will fail, eventually, but a lot of people would be sacrificed to the gods of money and control.

"Our problem is that we don't know a usable connection at the top. In short, we don't know who the top dog is, only the second and lower levels. We can't act effectively with the information we have at this time. If we don't get the top, it will just delay them, not stop them.

"I am acting independently at this time. I have known for some time that you are both intelligent and honest. You are a bit naive about international intrigue. You have the situation confused. I think you are capable of original thought.

"From this point, I'm lost. Do you feel you can, at least, cause a pause in the processes ... I'm scared. I don't want a bunch of bloody revolutions in all the countries here. I want China to become the world power, but I want it to happen without all the violence and pain."

"You know something? I think, just maybe, we can get them out of Panama. Beyond that, it will be up to you," Tony said. "You can get in touch with the three women?"

"Yes. Instantly."

"Can you arrange a meeting? One the ... other side ... can monitor with their electronic shit?"

"Perhaps. I think I can."

Clever Schemes

"I think you three are honest, and actually want to stop a bad thing," Tony said to Gina, Gilda, and Gloria. They were in a little restaurant just outside of Changuinola. "I think you will be safe if you are away from anyone who can use you.

"I can get you out of Panama, and that will stop at least part of what the hell ever they are trying to accomplish.

"Do you know anywhere, not in Panama, where you can say you're out of it and guarantee you won't get into it again? Anyone you can trust – and I mean more than Zamora. We can damned well tag his ass with you gone. We also can round up Vasquez, Samuels, Comacho, Arends, Guerra, Herrera, and several others. There's no doubt we can break one or more of them down. As long as they're here, that part will be easy.

"All I want from you is the names of any other who are in the upper levels. We know who the top one – or ones, in this case – are. The whole world does, really. It's a matter of proof, and that is coming into the time it won't matter. People are getting fed up with the bullshit. It will actually save some of their sorry asses, because they will have a focus, not just a family to attack.

"Agree?

"I certainly do!" Gina cried. "I can't spend the rest of my life hiding, and I'm not the small town girl type. Right now, there's not a city, or even small town in Panama where I would be safe for more than a week.

"You named the most important ones we found, with the exception of Menendez, Trotman, and Feilding."

"I'll take that deal! I know where I'll go!"

"Don't tell *anyone* where that is!" Sergio warned. She nodded.

"I'm in," Gilda said. "I can add the name Quintin. Enrique, I think. He's turned up a few places where I don't think he can explain."

"I can't leave for a little while. Maybe thirty seconds. Okay! Ready!" Gloria said.

They arranged with Sergio to leave immediately. They had brought the things they would need or want to keep. It would be dangerous for them to return to where they had been hiding.

They went to the waiting van and drove off. Mae Lum stepped from the next room to point outside. They went out.

"They heard everything in there. I don't know what you've accomplished, but you *did* get them out of Panama!"

She was an attractive woman, about 35 years old, Tony would estimate, and a superb actress.

"We'll monitor the border. They will not be stopped," Sergio explained. "They will, of course, offer bribes – that will be accepted. It would be beyond suspicious if they were detained for any reason."

"Yes," Tony added. "Do you know of Sr. Delgado, in Caracas?"

"Yes? He is a minor coordinator with the movement, and keeps exact tabs on which country is doing what to Venezuela."

"Among other things. He has arranged for the surveillance of our little group of international thugs."

"In Venezuela? I doubt that will prove of much importance," Mae said.

"If it was only Venezuela, I would agree. He's a lot more important than you know."

She raised an eyebrow, but didn't say anything more. They soon went their separate ways. Tony, back to his little piece of paradise, and Sergio back to Chiriqui Grande.

It had been six days since the meeting in Changuinola. Tony was out fishing, and had the radio on a local news station.

"... Maricaibo, Venezuela, last night around midnight. There were more than forty people, all of whom were suspected drug cartel leaders, and worse. Bankers who are suspected of laundering drug money, "Enforcers" for the cartels, and people who are suspected of human trafficking in the sexual market. There were no less than nine of them who were Panamanian, and many of them came regularly to Panama, or had temporary residences here, many in the Bocas and Chiriqui areas.

"Captain Valdez, Policia Nacional, said that one of the dead men was wanted for murder of a woman in Bocas. Punta Roballo area.

"It is believed the bombing was a result of a war among

the cartels."

Tony took out his cell phone to call Sergio, who said he was contacted about four in the morning because of the Zamora thing. Other than that, he didn't have a clue.

He called Mae. She said his clever little scheme to get them out of Panama had apparently caught them off guard, and they, except for Zamora, didn't have any place set to run to, so most of them went with him. They were all staying in the palace the head banker there owned. It set the coalition back, because he was going to run a central bank as soon as the economy recovered enough.

"He wasn't the head of it, but was on the second level. It shows that the attack was from someone on our side. Their side would very definitely not do anything that might slow getting a central bank there.

"We can but hope this will delay their plans for enough time to allow other interested parties who are not so violence prone to establish some kind of influential presence."

"Yes. We can but hope."

Two
<u>*Zenia*</u>

Zenia Crowley stretched, sighed, and poured a cup of the coffee from yesterday, made a face, and went into the study to check her e-mail.

7 spam/scams and two actual messages. Benny Santos wanted her to come to the Club Disquo with the band, who got a booking for a week. She could do a walk-on, and was guaranteed $100 plus a fifth of the tips.

Might do that one. She could use a hundred dollars for that dress in Stylistics!

She wrote back that she'd consider it. It was Friday night, so she was free.

The other was from Nando Vicente. For a date Saturday. Go to Changeleones.

Ugh! It was an international attraction, but, to her, was a river running over a big pile of rocks. Besides, she was going to Puerto Armuelles, so she could use that as an excuse. She liked Nando, but he wasn't any-body who would ever be more than an acquaintance.

She wrote: Sorry I can't make it. Already have a beach party I agreed to go to in P.A.

She decided to laze around for a little while, clean the apartment (it was getting a little too messy, even for her) then fix herself up for the club tonight. The silver-blue sheath. The split would show off her legs, and she had to admit she had great legs. The rest of her wasn't bad, by any definition. The type who hung around the disco were generally good people, but a few were just plain hoods. Hoods with a hell of a lot of money they couldn't explain, if they were ever asked. A few dollars here and there and they wouldn't be asked. She had once been given a tip of fifty dollars for a song. she figured the guy would want a little more than a song for that, and she wouldn't go for it, but he was gay, and had honestly liked the song and her voice. He had recorded it on his phone. He wanted to be her agent, but she didn't want any agent. He was very nice.

She had to do something with her hair. She hadn't gone for the cut and style this month, and it was getting frizzy. Maybe wear the wig. It was the way she usually had her hair when she performed.

She got a call from Aurelio Flores. He was nice enough, but thought he was the ultimate Latin Lover. He was fair, but a long way from special.

Nancy Gates called. About the beach party. Was she coming?

Well, she told Nando she was, and they were usually fun, so why not?

Jaime Serano called. He would be a really good lover – if he wasn't married. She told him, for the tenth time, she did *not* date married men. She dated gay men, now and then, but they weren't lying and cheating. If a man will cheat with you, he will cheat on you. Same with women. She wasn't going to ever be one of those.

Yvet called. Could she go with her to the hospital

Saturday to work with the children with cancer?

"I wish I could. I wish you had called yesterday, but I already made a date I can't break. I think it's wonderful, the good you are doing for those children!"

Beto Marseles called. Would she go with him to the club tonight?

"I'm going to be there, but with the band. I hope to see you!"

Not much else. Jorge, Donaldo, and Cisco called. Same kinds of things.

Benny greeted her when she came in the door. He said she was never to be charged cover, but they knew that. She performed there, so was considered a good friend and part time employee.

"You are a pure knock-out tonight! Gonzo is ready. Wait until the crowd is in the mood. You know the routine.

"You are really a knock-out!"

She did look good! Later, she happened to "accidentally" walk by the stage, and Gonzo called to come on up and say Hi! to everybody. She acted embarrassed, and went to the stage. Dino asked if she would do a number for them.

"Oh, but we haven't rehearsed, and my timing is so bad I'll screw it up!"

"*You* screw something up!? Your fans insist! Come on! For them!"

She acted embarrassed and went onto the stage, where Felipe put a spot on her. She acted like she was discussing what she would do with Gonzo, then went to pick up the broadcast mike to say, "I was writing a song with Gonz, but it isn't quite the way I want it, but he demands that I introduce it here tonight. Seeing he is co-writer, I guess I don't have a choice. I blame *him* for the parts I screw up!" She laughed and scanned the audience.

Beto started a beat with the bass, Dino came in on drums. Gonzo had the lead, and she picked a slightly syncopated rhythm on the acoustic guitar that just "happened" to be laying on a chair behind the mike. Naldo did a run on the keyboards, and she started: *Waiting on the dock. It's after eight o'clock, and I'm getting tired of always standing in the shade of your demands.*

So listen to me well, the thing I have to tell you won't be delayed another day.

The message isn't hard to do, to mine own self I must be true. It's over. It was fun. But you aren't the one.

So let's be clear, I'm not your "dear" for you to play

Goodbye! Have fun! It's just begun. It was over long before we ever met.

In short, the one I need has not appeared quite yet. I won't be here to greet you when you fin'ly show.

Bye now! I'll find another much like you. It's the same mistake I seem to always do.

It just wasn't going to work. It was corny. It, frankly, stunk to high heaven!

But the crowd loved it. The story of her life in music. Do a piece of utter trash like that, hate it, and have to do it everywhere you go for years!

Not this time! "Now, *that* one didn't work at all! I apologize for putting you through it. I *won't* be finishing it!"

They loved it even more for that, but she was *not* doing it again!

"I guess that's part of the biz. Everybody tries something that, looking back, they were mortified for doing.

"So! I said I'd do one, but didn't think it would be that one. I owe you something with a little bit of lyric that you can appreciate.

"Gonz, Dino? How about *Lost Dreams*?"

She did the number. It brought the house down, so to speak.

Nilsa, the waitress, brought her a note. It had a hundred dollar bill in it. *I'll be at Sandy's.*

She hadn't seen anyone there she knew who would do that. What was going on? Nilsa said a very handsome *hunk* sent it, but he left.

She looked thoughtful. She didn't know who ... but she was used to this kind of thing. She was no puta, but Nilsa said he was a hunk.

Maybe, but not for money. She would go to Sandy's to see what this was about. Surely someone who Nilsa described as a hunk wouldn't be looking for paid sex. Unless he was the one being paid. There were plenty of male prostitutes around, but they preyed on the older ugly women.

Curiouser and curiouser!

<u>Meeting Marko</u>

Sandy's was full, but it usually was on Saturday night late. Zenia looked over the crowd, and immediately saw a very attractive man sitting at a little table on the side of the bandstand. He stood up and smiled. She felt a little tingle. He *was* damned attractive!

"Ah! Miss Crowley! Please join me!" His voice was a smooth baritone - *from six words? What's the matter with me!?*

"I don't ... I just came because I'm curious. What's going on?"

"I'm called Marko Slade, here. I have a little proposition for you. I think you are more than qualified for it."

Uh-oh! A proposition? Please let it not be that! "Oh?"

"I am working with an international investigation agency – don't look at me like that. It is *not* CIA! They're a joke!"

"I've run across a few of them. They're a very unfunny joke around here. Totally incompetent."

"Incompetent is an understatement. We're investigating things more on the economic line."

"Counterfeit? I know there's a lot of it here, but it's easy to ignore, because it's dollars, and they're phony money to start with."

"That's not our target. It's tied in, because it's financing a lot of little rebellions."

"Get to the point. Tell me what you want, and I'll agree

or say to shove it up your ass."

"It *is* dangerous. Several have already been murdered. It has to do with central banks."

"Rothschilds? I've heard a lot about that, but don't think it means as much as they want it to mean. The indios here don't even have money, and are a hell of a lot better off than we are. It's like the bogus shit. Who cares? It spends the same. You just have to know where to spend it – or get change for it. Money is just numbers in a computer somewhere. That's what people are learning, and they're sick and tired of the bullshit, more and more."

"You've expressed the same before, which is why I think you'll help in this.

"You have to remain secret. I've gone through a lot to not be seen talking with you. They don't know about me, and I don't want them to become suspicious. It's, as I've said, dangerous.

"I think you'd like the danger part. You seem ... bored, even when you're performing."

She laughed. "You just don't know! The games I have to play to fit their fantasies! I have to look like a bimbo idiot sex object, and they love my music. Shake my ass and sell a couple hundred more CDs. It's sickening, but I've found I'm spoiled enough that I like to sell those extra CDs so I can get that special dress that looked so great in the window, but isn't that great when you get it home.

"You do know women get the extra sexy, slinky, slit-up-the-leg gown to make other women jealous, don't you? We hope men will like it, but they like anything.

"What do I do? I would like to get you in bed, but I won't

do that kind of thing for any other reason. I'm not a whore. I know I'll get paid for the work, but private stuff isn't work."

His turn to laugh. "I agree. No pay for the extra-curricular things.

"It's mainly finding out who is really in charge in certain areas. We know most of the underlings frequent places where you appear, but would move you to better class places. Those people have money up the ass, and go to more 'presentable' places. You've already established that you perform because you like it, and aren't on the sleep-your-way-to-the-top train. If you were that, you'd be a star right now, instead of a local big attraction.

"You know El Critico, in Puerto Armuelles?"

"It's a high-class brothel. I've been there. Very good food, as well as other feature attractions."

"And some of the shows, those not local, have no connection, other than performing in the show. Some of the major attractions appear there. As I said, it is already established that your interest is only in the show, not the side-cars.

"We'll have some very professional, known promoters. You'll get class material – not like that silly thing you dumped at the disco tonight.

"Was the one about dreams your own? It was damned good!"

"Yes. I'll want to write most of my own stuff. It would be good to have professional orchestration. I always wanted to have back-up like Shakira and Ana Gabriel. I think I have the talent to pull if off."

"I do, too! Well, would you like to have a drink before we go to the hotel?"

"No. We can go to my place. No need to pay for rooms when I have them already, bought and paid for!"

"Sounds like a plan. It will save us having to meet somewhere for a briefing and all that."

"Yeah. Nobody's watching. Yet."

"We can work this thing fairly well like that," Gordon Nolan, head coordinator for "The Project" said. "We can show you all we have about certain people, and you can be the stupid sex-queen bimbo sitting there without a clue while they discuss other people. You speak English and Portugese, which they will use to keep you from accidentally hearing anything important.

"Bill Bergston is already known as a good agent/manager for soft rock and pop. He likes the Wall-of-Sound orchestration – which I have to say you don't need. You have the voice.

"You can meet with him this afternoon and put something together. You're good at sponty, so it can be a stroke of luck that you're visiting a friend in Puerto when the band that's booked gets food poisoning or something. And on Friday night! Oh, alas! What will we do?! We have all these clients who are expecting a name act! Alas!"

Zenia gave him the finger. "And this ditzy dingbat with a good voice just happens to be staying three squares away, and she has performed with that band from Mexico who were to appear at the disco, but would have to play regaton and bachata – that they don't know any of!"

"Mexican band?" Marko asked.

"Yeah. I played with them a couple of times in David and once in Bocas. They really do have a tentative locally, and don't want to play it, but need the money. They're good. For this 'accidental' type of thing, we could spend a couple of hours going over things I do."

"Well, it's Wednesday. Could you be ready to do a sponty Friday?" Gordy asked.

"Plenty of time."

"Then let's do it!"

El Critico

"Ladies and gentlemen, we have the sad news to deliver that Los Victimos is suffering from food poisoning, and can't appear tonight." There were groans from the audience.

"The good news is that the popular favorite, Zenia, is, by good fortune, staying with friends here [A couple of people clapping], along with Tacos por Todos, from Mexico, who have just refused a gig at the disco because they do not do regaton and such noise."

There was some tentative clapping.

"For tonight – and maybe more, please welcome ZeniaTacos!"

The lights came on on the stage, where a mariachi band [plus key-boards and drums] was shown. They started a song by La Quinta Estacion, *El Sol no Regresa*. Zenia came to the mike to perform the blistering rock number. It was a huge success. She immediately went into *Suenos de Amor*, one of her own numbers, that was even bigger, followed with *Yo Te Amo*. Two numbers later, it was certain that no one cared if Los Victimos never came back.

At the break, she went to sit at a table with an older couple who had seen her in David, they said. She talked politely, and thanked them for their kind words, then moved toward the bar, where one of the girls who worked there was waiting for her "date" to come out of the baños.

She seemed to have some unpleasant words with that one, then went to the bar to ask for a Tanquerey and tonic. A somewhat fat and somewhat vulgar man said he'd pay for the drink. She said the drinks were part of the job, but thanks.

"You got a great sound. I never heard but one of those songs before."

"Why, thank you! We haven't worked together much. I just found out they needed someone here, and had the time, but made it very plain I worked for the show, not the other ... things ... about this place. I have nothing against a girl making the best of what she has, but my singing is enough."

"Yeah. Nita said that. I ain't tryin' to pick you up here, 'cause you wouldn't. You got class.

"I'm Jorge Smith. Papa was a Brit in the zone, and Mama's pure Panameño, but her Papa was from here and her Mama was from Colombia. I'm in produce. Vegetables for the market, you know. Send bananas to everywhere. That kind of vegetables, mostly."

"I'm just a lazy spoiled brat who lucked out with a good voice, so I don't have to work much. Singing isn't like work.

"Oh! There's that doctor who can cure cancer and like that! I know two people where it worked! He could get millions, but just gives it away free!

"Oh, shucks! I have to get back to the stage. We haven't done much together, so I don't know what to do, so I'll just, as we say in showbiz, have to wing it. I hope I'm not too bad. If they want us to stay, we can work up a list.

"Mucho gusto!" She headed for the stage. That went well! First break, and she met one of the ones to investigate. She hoped she had come across as a bit stupid and naive.

She did six numbers, and the band did a couple of instrumentals. She thought about going into the audience during the instrumentals, then decided it would be better to play rhythm on the guitar.

Another one she was to check out came in during the show and went to talk with Jorge, so there was already a connection. They knew each other and, as suspected, met there to not be noticed.

At the break, she went to the bar and ordered another gin and tonic. She giggled at Jorge, and said she had to be careful, because she got drunk too easy. She giggled again.

"It doesn't seem to get in the way on the stage," the second man said. "I'm Jaime Jones. Call me Jim. Jorge, here, was a neighbor in the zone when we were growing up."

"Oh, nothing bothers me when I'm up there. I can be so drunk I don't know where I am, out here. Up there, everything's tranquilo."

"Do you appear many places around here?" he asked – in English. She looked blank. He asked in Spanish.

"Oh, [giggle] some in David and Bocas and like that. They wanted me to go to Panama City for a test for making CDs, but I don't want that because you don't even have a life of your own anymore.

"He really just wanted to get in my pants, I think. If he hadn't tried that kind of line, I might've. He was sorta sexy.

"Oh! I'm awful! [giggle]"

"I can see why! You're better looking than anyone else here – and it's a whorehouse – and they're professionals!" Jorge said. "If I thought I had a chance, I'd spend all my time trying to get a date!"

"Oh, silly! Why wouldn't you have the same chance as anyone else?" [giggle]

He laughed. "I have a mirror. Some of the guys here could turn *me* on! Nobody like you would even look at me twice!"

"Oh, silly! If all a girl looks at is, like that, there wouldn't be but two guys in here! Other things are more important!"

They chatted and she acted just a little drunker, then went to the stage for the final segment. It was as popular as the first two, and was mostly repeating things they requested.

Now what? Would it be smart to talk to Jorge and Jim again?

No. She talked with a couple of people, turned down an offer of $250 for an hour, and she and the band left.

She had met two of the four people she was supposed to learn anything she could about. Jim had called as they were leaving that he'd see them tomorrow. Great show!

Well, tomorrow and tomorrow. She'd see what developed.

She went into town to shop, where she met several people she'd seen last night. She had certainly been a hit! It was almost embarrassing when they kept on with the praise. It had been a very lucky accident that Tacos was there. She meshed well with them, and they didn't know her well enough to know she wasn't half-way to an idiot. She would spend the afternoon rehearsing a few more numbers. Bill would be there to give the band a few pointers about the sound she wanted. It seemed he was fair at many instruments, but was better at arrangement. He took a couple of her more heavy numbers and showed them how to make the wall of sound method work for her. He also brought a subliminal beat generator that worked on sound that was just below hearing.

She was leaving the session when Jim came to say it was great that he caught her! He insisted that he would buy her the best dinner in Chiriqui. She said she had to eat early so she could be ready for the show. They would meet at six, she could have the meal, and would have plenty of time to make the show at nine.

He took her to a little restaurant out on the peninsula a ways, where she was served what really *was* the best meal she had tasted in a long time! When they were leaving, the third man she was supposed to investigate was coming in. Jim introduced her to Tomas Vilasquez a major partner in the big import-export company in Frontera. Vilasquez was with a very sexy, if stiff [she was outclassed all the way, and knew it] woman in her thirties. Vanesa Ranchero.

The show was a bigger hit that night than the night before. Roberto Camos, manager of El Critico, asked if she could appear Sunday afternoon. They generally only had a pianist, but she was such a hit they would pay her double for Sunday afternoon until whenever. Virginia Rios, owner, came to say they would like a contract, long term.

She would consider it.

Rios was possibly involved. Zenia acted excited and said it was a dream come true! People actually *did* like her music!

The Sunday show was even bigger. She was glad she took this job as a lark.

She met Arnie Daniels, an agent for the big CD company. He wanted to interview her for a contract. Rios said she should sign the contract with El Critico first. It would give her a bargaining point!

This was getting out of hand! Rios and Daniels wanted a meeting with her tomorrow at noon. She pulled the ditzy act, and said, darn! She had to practice all day tomorrow, but she could maybe meet on Tuesday. Or Wednesday. She had to have time to think or she would do something stupid. and she had to finish writing a song that just popped into her head like magic!

She finally got away from them and went to the house she was staying in. Anita, the girl she had words with in El Critico [who passed on the instructions from Marko] and Bill were there. They spent some time making what plans they could. Anita said to be extra careful. She overheard Jim and Jorge saying they had to check her out. She was the perfect type to be seen with, and would explain why they spent so much time at El Critico.

"And that some people were due here soon, so it would give them a reason to be seen with them, too. Everyone enamored by the sexy singer.

"They said they had to be sure you didn't know much about them. The one called Jim said he already showed you don't speak English, so that wouldn't be a problem. He said you weren't the brightest star in the galaxy."

They talked a bit longer, then Bill and Anita went out through the woods behind the house and back into town.

Who was coming from somewhere else that they needed an excuse to be seen in the same place? Was this timed better than planned – or worse?

Zenia wanted to appear just a local girl who had a good voice and was getting a break – and who wasn't exactly a genius. She took her digital camera and went to the muelle, where she was stopped and it was explained that she was the only one responsible if she went out on the dock, because it was in poor repair.

"Oh! They told me that! It's why I'm wearing flats!"

The two guards looked at each other. One shrugged. "Flats?"

"Yeah! It would be stupid to wear heels on the muelle. All those loose boards to dump you on your ass!

"I'm Zenia. I'm a singer at El Critico!"

"Er, *El Critico*? You don't look like ... I mean ... *El Critico*?"

She laughed. "Just a singer. I'm not a puta – but I don't see anything wrong if you have to do that to make a living. I only do it for fun or because the guy's special, you know?"

"Dios mio!" the other blurted. "You could make a thousand dollars a night! Easy! ... I'm ... desculpame! You're a true beauty!?

"Oh, silly. I make plenty just singing, and I don't have to

pretend some pig turns me on.

"I don't have time to be here at sunset, and I work until two, so can't get up for the sunrise. Elena has some of the most fantastic pictures!

"I'll be careful. I may not be really smart, but I know to be careful in places like this." She spotted Rios standing behind a big hibiscus across the street. She waved at the guards and went on out on the muelle.

She saw Rios talking to the guards when she was halfway out. She grinned to herself.

Why was Rios checking on her? Just jealous, or deeper than that?

She went out, talked with a couple of the Indios fishing there, took some more pictures, and headed back to town.

Bill and Marko were at her place. She asked about Rios.

"Rios? Virginia Rios? Isn't she that Mexican Mafia connection? Owns a hunk of Critico? Is she here in Panamá?" Bill asked. "We have to know what's going on! Jaime, Colombia, Jorge, here, Velasquez, Argentina, Flores, Brasil ... I don't like this. At *all*!"

"Rios' group does *not* much like the others. If they manage to consolidate ... this could get very hairy, very fast. It's too soon! we aren't ready!"

"They don't ... Maybe they want you to *think* they don't like each other?" Zenia suggested. "What's too soon?"

"They might have more resources than we know, which is why we needed you. It's paid off, in a way, but it might be hard to counter them this soon." Bill replied. "We have to do something to slow this down! We *have* to!"

They spent some time discussing what they could do.

Zenia said she had to practice with the band, but she may be able to do something to make them slow down. If they were suspicious of each other – and that seemed sure! – they would want to check some things before they got in too deep. "I read a lot of those spy books. I have an idea.

"Marko, do you have a name or two I could mention when I was too drunk to know what I was doing?"

"I'll find one or two before tonight. We have a couple of people watching the Mexican connection. We didn't think they were in it much, but we've been wrong before."

Zenia went to practice. As she hoped, Jim was there when she left the studio, and asked if she would like to meet him and a couple of friends for dinner. She had met some of them. He wanted to show her off!

"Silly! We're just good friends! I'm going with Arnie, so I don't fool around, I mean, unless he does, then it's okay for me, too! Equal rights!" She giggled.

She got a leer that was as pointed as anything she ever saw. She acted like it didn't register. "I don't have to sing tonight, so I can party a little, but not too much, and only so far."

"Anybody who would fool around on somebody like you would be a total idiot – or gay!"

"Oh, I have a lot of gay friends. We don't do much that way, but we can tell each other all our dirty secrets. They can ask me what turns on a guy, and they told me lots of things that guys get turned on with. I know how you guys get turned on when a girl – or gay – nibbles at your tits, even though you really don't have tits.

"We won't go to El Critico, I hope. I don't want to go

there except to sing with the band. Some of the girls get mad because I'm there. I never could figure that out."

"We can go to Aimee's again. They do have the best food here, and it's more a private club. I like to be with the sexiest girl there!"

She giggled. "Silly!

"I have to fix my face and get into better clothes. Six o'clock, at my place?"

"Perfect! I'll be there!"

She waved and went on toward her friend's house. Strange that he knew where it was!

She had watched his expression change while she rattled on about her gay "friends." There was a mirror on the shelf. He rolled his eyes at one point, and she had a hard time not laughing in his face. When she said that about nibbling on his tits, he had grabbed his crotch.

Brother! Even talking about it got him horny!

He was more certain than ever she was an airheaded bimbo. *That* was perfect!

"This is Pepe Flores, a business partner," Jim introduced. "He's from Brasil. He doesn't like people here to know, but he owns three big banks!"

"Mucho gusto!" Zenia repled. "I knew a guy who owned a bank before. He didn't want anyone to know, but told me. He said people thought bankers were all millionaires, but he was the only one he knew who really was."

"I think I saw you this morning on the old dock?" Rios said. "You have to be careful. It's a dangerous place to be." She stared hard at Zenia, who acted as though it went over her head.

"Well, they need to fix it in places. You could fall and twist you ankle, and like that.

"You talk like Mexico! Are you from there?"

Rios looked confused. "Yes. I am in business in Mexico City."

"I didn't like Mexico City. It's dirty and loud and all the Mexican guys hit on me all the time.

"I mean, I don't mind, so much, and a couple would be dreams, but ... well, it's socially acceptable there.

"Do you know Bertrando Dar ... er, I plain forgot his name! You wouldn't know him, anyway. There are millions of people in Mexico City! [Rios looked like she had been slapped in the face with a wet fish. Zenia didn't notice.]

"Jorge, you really look good in a suit! Like a big businessman or a lawyer!"

"He is a big businessman – and a lawyer!" Pepe said. "They have Chateau Briand tonight! I recommend it!"

They chatted a bit. Soon, Zenia was left out of the conversation, which shifted into English. She learned a bit about them, while acting like she was a bit miffed that she wasn't the center of attention. She had a second wine, and acted a little drunk ... when she let another name slip, then covered quickly. She saw Rios give Pepe a very hard look when she mentioned Liam, er, Something, from France, or somewhere, who was staying in Panamá City last ... er, she didn't like Panamá City any more than she liked Mexico City or Bogota. They were just cities, and cities were all the same.

Later, when she was being ignored, for the most part, she overheard Rios and Flores having an argument on the veranda.

"The stupid is an act! She's working for someone! I think LeSeur or Darmila – or both! She's ... I don't get it!" Rios cried. "She could fuck up the whole deal if they're trying ... we have to know more about her! How did she get in with Smith and Jones – other than using those names is a dead giveaway that's something's up!"

"I don't think I like being here. At *all*! There's definitely something happening. If they're behind it, our asses are about to need some heavy duty lubrication!"

"If they're behind it – either bunch – we're going to need burial insurance!"

"This is hell! We have to protect ourselves!"

Watch Your Back!

"Something is happening! I don't know what the *hell* is going on!" Marko cried. "Rios has two people on the way from Mexico City. They're what they call 'muscle' or 'enforcers' there!

"What in *hell* is going on!?"

"I heard the Flores character on the phone," Anita said. "He said to check up, fast and complete, on all the others."

"And Smith and Jones have asked the same things, and have a man from Panamá City coming here to keep an eye on things. Everyone is having their hit men come here," Bill said. "Something has come up that has them all ready to cut everyone else's throats!"

"Well, I was all confused and was a little pouty because I was being ignored, and they said the party was for *me*!" Zenia said, innocently. "I mean, they all were talking in English or French or like that, and I didn't have a *clue* what they were talking about, and it was just *rude*!"

Marko grinned. "And you just happened to ask why somebody said something about somebody else?"

"Well, no, silly! I was a little drunk and asked about somebody named Bertrando ... Somebody – I remembered *just then* I wasn't supposed to talk about, so I cleverly said I didn't like Mexico City, because it was loud and dirty, which made them not even notice I said anything! Then a man called Liam – I was a little too drunk, and wasn't thinking that I wasn't to ever mention him either – so I did the clever thing, and nobody even knew I ever said his name!"

Bill and Anita gave her the finger. Marko laughed, and said, "In other words, silly little airheaded bimbo, you, lit a match that has turned into an inferno! *Love* it!

"You said you'd slow them down. I didn't think you would make them come to an emergency stop!"

"You should have seen the look on Rios' face when I mentioned Bertrando, er, Somebody! The hardest part was not to laugh in her face, right then and there!"

They all laughed, then Bill said, "It's funny as hell, but it's serious as hell, at the same time. We can't predict what they'll do."

"If it's like the book I was reading last month, they'll be so busy looking at each other they won't dare do anything else," Zenia said. "I have to admit this has turned out good for me, so far. The recording contract is real.

"Now, I have to decide if what I told Jim is true. Do I want that, with all that goes with it? Would it make life better, or would it put me in a prison I can't get out of?"

Gordon Nolan got out of a cab out front, and rushed in. "What in *hell* is going on here!?" he demanded. "My god! It looks like a cartel war on the horizon! Hit men from four countries and this one? *Why*? What the *fuck* is going on with you idiots!"

"Hi, Gordy!" Zenia cried, in her bimbo voice. "I was just talking with those hoody types last night, at a party that was *supposed* to be for me, and forgot I wasn't to ever say names like Bertrando, er, I don't like Mexico City. It's dirty and too loud, and Liam LeSeu..., er, I don't like Bogota and those either!

"I get silly when I'm drunk! Is there anywhere to dance around here? I don't mean the disco. That's just noise. I'll have another gin and tonic [giggle]."

"You didn't!"

"Well, it was *supposed* to be a party for *me*, and they just *ignored* me and talked in some foreign language! It was just *rude*!"

"Christ! Will they get together and go after LeSeur and Company, or will he get word and go after them? We have to figure this out!"

"Why?" Zenia asked.

"What ...?"

"Either way, your problem is solved. Sit back, have a beer, and enjoy!"

Marko looked thoughtful, then burst out laughing. "You're a genius! Will you marry me?"

"Oh, I'm not for marrying anyone. Let's just keep living together until it gets boring."

They laughed again – and went to Josy's for a beer.

"... body of a Mexican businesswoman who owned a night club in Puerto Armuelles and those of three of her partners in a vegetable distribution company, and one a lawyer for a bank, were found on the beach at the base of the muelle at dawn this morning. Police do not know the motive of the murders, but feel it may be connected to the drug cartels in Colombia.

"Vanesa, I have said before that it is not intelligent to

become involved with those people."

"Yes, Eduardo, you have. I have heard you say exactly that on many occasions when we in the news business have to report on their sordid violences. You have ... what? [a mumbled voice from off-camera. A man handed her a sheet of paper. She read it, looked shocked, and continued.] I have just been handed a notice that two other people who were associated with the bodies at the muelle had what was obviously a staged accident, in which their automobile ended up in the Mud River. Police say they know it was no accident, that a bullet in the head was not from running off the highway.

"We do not want or need those types of people ... what? [a repeat of the mumbled voice and paper] Well! Two men who what were known as hit men shot and killed each other near Manaca!

"Ed, this is getting out of hand! Drug wars? *Here*? In Puerto Armuelles?"

"I just received a noticia from Panamá City," Eduardo replied. "A Sr. Liam LeSeur, known to be associated with the dead people here through banking interests, was shot from a moving car on the Via Espania there. He was not even suspected of drug cartel connections. He was a major executive in the banking business.

"Vanesa, this is going to be a puzzle for years, I think! *No* one knows of any connection ... so there may be none ... but it is far to much of a coincidence. *No* one can figure this one!"

Marko turned the TV off. "Not quite! *We* know of the connection! C'mere, woman!"

Three
<u>*Maria*</u>

Matilde Sanchez Rivera, medicine woman for the comarca, Cusapin, Comarca Ngobe Bugle, watched the cayuca leave the dock to head for Chiriqui Grande.

One of those estraneros would not return. It was indefinite which one, or she would have warned them [though they would have ignored her, as long experience had shown]. It could be either of two. One was very evil and the other, while not evil, was no prize specimen.

She shook her head and went back to her house by the river.

Should she tell the famous detective down the beach about it?

No. He couldn't change fate on this one, and he was very old.

There was too much red in the clouds this sunrise. There was gold, too. That was not a good combination. Blood and gold in the same omen. She had seen that before.

So! It would be the woman who would not return.

She went inside to fix her breakfast.

"A woman, Maria Dehammer, went to Cusapin with you. She returned to Chidiqui Grande with you. You then left Chiriqui Grande for Cusapin with her. You arrived at

Cusapin without her. Her body was found a couple of kilometers from here. She had been strangled and thrown into the sea. No one but you was anywhere near her at the time," Capitan Nito Faraday said to George Bantine. "We don't need a genius or better on this one.

"Why? What was it about?"

Bantine sighed. "It was spur of the moment. I didn't plan to kill her."

"This is the comarca. We look at things a bit differently. Tell me about it. Matilde will tell me if what you say its true, and if you are hiding part of it. She has already said you are devious, but not about the murder."

"She was blackmailing me. She was going to take everything! I lost my temper!"

"What was she blackmailing you about? That is something we consider here."

"I ... can't tell you."

"The gold," Matilde said.

"Gold?" Nito asked.

"Yes. He has some gold. She was going to take it."

"There's plenty of gold here. That isn't something to kill anyone for," Nito pointed out.

"It was *my* gold! She was going to take it!"

"You found it on the comarca?" Nito asked.

"I ... won't say."

"Why?"

"Why? What do you mean, *why*? All it would mean is that *you* take it instead! It's not fair! *I* found it!"

"Why would I take it? Why would I want it?"

"It's *gold*!"

"It's a pretty metal to make trinkets of. There's quite a lot of it on the comarca. There are large deposits near Buabidi and Quebrada Tula. When we want to buy something in the cities, we will take some to trade for money. It's not good for much else.," Nito said. "I have a carved gold horse that weighs more than twenty pounds sitting on a shelf at home."

"You speak better English than I do! You have an education! You know very damned well that it's worth a lot of money! You don't fool me with this 'Oh, gee! Is it really worth so much' shit!"

"It's worth very little here," Matilde said, quietly. "You don't understand the comarca or my people. To us, you are a silly fool chasing a dream that will never be anything more than a dream."

"I know what you are thinking," Nito explained."You are looking at it from the POV of the greed society. It has no application here. Nobody cares if you found some gold. All we ask is that you don't tell anyone outside where you found it. We don't need the headaches having a bunch of your type running around would cause.

"I order you off he comarca, and you may never return. Your little murder was for nothing. If Panamá wants to pursue it, that's their concern, not ours. If she was blackmailing you, she has shown herself to also be a criminal of an intolerable type.

"You have four hours to be off the comarca. If you ever return, you will be declared outlaw, and anyone may kill you.

"Matilde, you agree that is fair?"

"Yes. His gold will form a prison around him, where he may never trust anyone, because they may be like him. He will never know inner peace. He is a very sad person. You will allow him to take the gold he has collected, and he will take it, and he will regret it for the rest of his life. Because of it, he will never know love. He will not own the gold. The gold will own him, and make him its slave.

"Are you and Nicole going to be at the gathering this afternoon?"

"Yes. Thank you, Matilde. The people appreciate your talent and caring."

"That's *it*?!" George cried.

"What?" Nito asked.

"You mean ... I admit I killed the bitch, you say it means I have to get off the comarca, and I can even take the gold?!"

"You are guilty of extreme stupidity. That is, in itself, not called a crime here. You can take as much gold as you can carry, no more."

"I have fourteen pounds seven ounces! That's more than a hundred fifty thousand dollars! I could have carried it out, all along?!"

"Matilde told us what would happen. You will take it, and her predictions will come true. She has never been known to be wrong.

"My father is a famous detective. He established the "what you can carry" policy [Clint Faraday Mysteries #33: Die Trying]. You aren't capable of understanding our culture, our value system.

"You now have a little more than three hours to be off

the comarca."

"Are you going to report that I killed Maria to the Panamanian police?"

"No. Why would I? Matilde told you, very clearly, what you sentence will be."

"She did?"

Nito sighed. "Just go, okay?"

George left. Nito walked along the beach to his father's old house – where he was staying – to find Clint and Tyna there. They had a place on a nearby island now.

"Well! I saw you were with Matilde!" Tyna said. "Not a case, was it?"

"Not a difficult one. Gold and murder."

"That the killer found wasn't illegal for him or her to have, all along?" Clint asked.

"Uh-huh."

"Pathetic!"

C. D. Moulton's works are available on most major outlets as printed or e-books. CD writes the CD Grimes, PI, mysteries, the Det. Lt. Nick Storie mysteries, the Clint Faraday mysteries, the Flight of the Maita science fiction series, books on orchid culture and many others of many types. Mystery, adventure, intrigue, science fiction, humor, fantasy, paranormal, mild erotica, and factual.

www.ingramcontent.com/pod-product-compliance
Lightning Source LLC
Chambersburg PA
CBHW050608160726
48003CB00003B/1103